Eddie Alan Freed

eter Potato

rk Marrow

Radish

Polly
Pomegranate

Tim Tomato

D1624148

The Garden Gang
stories and pictures by

Jayne Fisher

Twelve year old **Jayne Fisher** is the youngest ever Ladybird author. She was only nine years old when she wrote these charming stories about fruit and vegetable characters.

Writing and drawing aren't Jayne's only interests. She has studied for the ribbon awards of the Royal School of Church Music, and plays the classical guitar and the recorder. Jayne sews, bakes, reads avidly, plays chess and keeps two gerbils and breeds stick insects.

But it is perhaps her own little garden at home which gave her the ideas for these stories. Jayne's bold, colourful felt-tipped pen illustrations are bound to appeal to young children and we can all learn a few lessons from the characters in the 'Garden Gang'.

Percival Pea

Ladybird Books Loughborough

A scatterbrain,
that's what Percival Pea was,
a round, plump,
jolly, lovable, scatterbrain.
He had lots of friends
and they all thought
the world of him.

But really,
he did some of the most
extraordinarily peculiar things.
One day, as he sat eating
a gigantic cream bun,
he suddenly decided
to watch tennis
on television.
He carefully put his bun
on his chair and
went over to switch on.

Well, you can all guess
what happened next,
can't you?
That's right, he sat
on his lovely cream bun.

9

Another time, he went upstairs
to run his bath water,
then ambled
out of the bathroom.
"Now, what did I
come upstairs for?"
he asked himself.
"Oh, I know, my sun-hat."
He went to get it
and then hurried out
to do some gardening.

Eventually,
after two hours or so,
he came indoors.
Hot water was dripping
through the ceiling!
Then he remembered
about his bath.
He certainly was
a scatterbrain.

13

He often used to invite
friends to stay
and then go off fishing
for the day.

But things began
to get serious
when one day,
he forgot to get up.

17

So his friends
held a meeting
to decide what to do.
It was Robert Raspberry
who suggested
that knots in his
handkerchief
might help.
So they bought him
a large , blue-spotted
handkerchief
and told him
to remember things,
by tying knots
in the corners.

But that was no good
because he could not
remember what he had tied
the knots for.

A few days later
Roger Radish came up
with the idea, that
if they bought
Percival a diary,
and he kept it
on his bedside table,
he could write in it
everything he wanted
to remember.

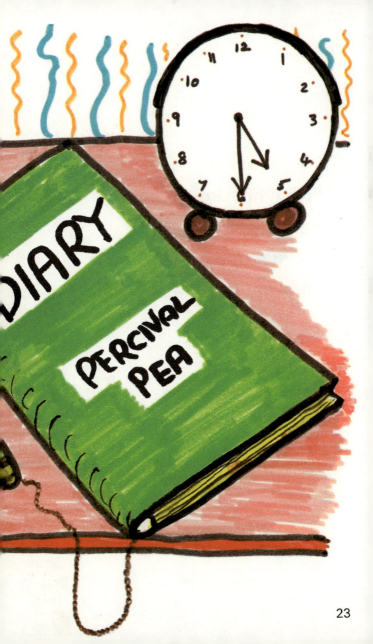

From that day to this,
Percival Pea
is still round, plump,
jolly and lovable.

But he is no longer a scatterbrain!

Polly
Pomegranate

Polly Pomegranate
loved to dance.
She never walked anywhere.
She always twirled,
twisted, skipped,
leapt or waltzed along,
and nobody
took any notice of her
because they were all
so used to her prancings.

Now our story starts
when the Fruit and
Vegetable People became
very worried about
the state of the greenhouse.
Panes of glass were broken
and the door was hanging
off its hinges.
"Something
has to be done,"
they said, "and quickly,
before the winter comes."

Tim Tomato
was certainly not
his usual jolly self
and Colin Cucumber
was downright miserable,
for they both knew that
the repairs would be costly.
"However can we
make enough money?"
they wondered, miserably.

Just then, Polly Pomegranate
came dancing by,
in her usual graceful manner.
"Hello," she said, sweetly.
"Is anything wrong?"
"The greenhouse
is falling to bits,"
said Peter Potato, gruffly.
"It will cost lots
of money to mend it."
"Oh dear!" said Polly.
"Is there anything
I can do to help?"

It was then
that Colin Cucumber had
his brilliant brainwave.
"How about holding
a concert on the lawn,
and letting Polly
dance for everyone?
We could charge people
to come and see her.
We'd make a lot of money
that way," he said.

Everyone thought
it was a splendid idea
and quickly started
to help with
the arrangements.
Some made posters,
some found boxes
for seats.

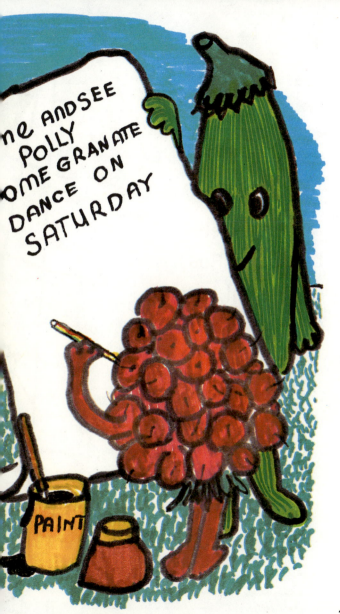

ne ANDSEE
POLLY
OME GRANATE
DANCE ON
SATURDAY

PAINT

Sally Spider
busied herself
by making Polly
a beautiful
silken ballet dress.

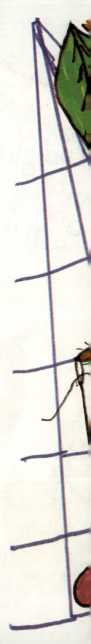

The Caterpillar twins
made her a soft, furry cape
from their old
cast-off skins,
and Felicity Foxglove
provided her with
a pair of pink ballet shoes.

When the great day came
the garden was full
of excited people,
all waiting to see
lovely Polly Pomegranate.
Her friends were
so proud of her,
because she danced
as she had never
danced before.
How they all cheered
and clapped!

When the visitors
had all gone home,
and Peter Potato
was counting up the money
they had collected,
he found that they had
enough to repair
the greenhouse
and some over.

Do you know
what they did
with the spare money?
They sent Polly
to Ballet School
and you can guess
what she became,
can't you?
Yes, she became
what she had always
wanted to be . . .

A famous ballerina!

Colin Cucumber

Penelope
Strawberry

Percival Pea

Oliver Onion

00507